Copyright © 2009 by NordSüd Verlag AG, CH-8005 Zürich, Switzerland.
First published in Switzerland under the title *Der Regenbogenfisch entdeckt die Tiefsee*.
English translation copyright © 2009 by NorthSouth Books Inc., New York 10016.

First published in the United States, Great Britain, Canada, Australia, and New Zealand in 2009
by NorthSouth Books Inc., an imprint of NordSüd Verlag AG, CH-8005 Zürich, Switzerland.
Distributed in the United States by NorthSouth Books Inc., New York 10016.
First paperback edition published in Great Britain in 2011.

Library of Congress Cataloging-in-Publication Data is available.
Printed in China by ColorPrint Offset, November 2014

ISBN: 978-0-7358-2248-1 (trade edition).
10 9 8 7 6 5 4 3 2
ISBN: 978-0-7358-4066-9 (paperback edition).
10 9 8 7 6 5 4 3

www.northsouth.com
Meet Marcus Pfister at www.marcuspfister.ch

Marcus Pfister

RAINBOW FISH
DISCOVERS THE
DEEP SEA

North
South

A long way out in the deep blue sea, Rainbow Fish and his friends played happily near an underwater canyon. Over the edge, the seabed dropped deep down. No one knew how far.

"I would love to know what's down there," said Rainbow Fish to the little blue fish. "Who knows what's waiting to be discovered?"

"If I were you, I'd stay up here," said the octopus. "I've heard that it's cold down there, and dark—and full of strange creatures nothing like us."

So Rainbow Fish had to be content to swim along the edge and stare down into the depths, wondering what was there.

One day a strong ocean current pulled Rainbow Fish's last sparkling silver scale right off. The scale drifted over the edge of the canyon wall and sank down and down and down into the darkness.

Rainbow Fish wanted to chase after it, but the little blue fish pulled him back. "No, Rainbow Fish!" he cried. "Please don't go after it. There are strange creatures down there."

"I'd like to meet them," said Rainbow Fish.

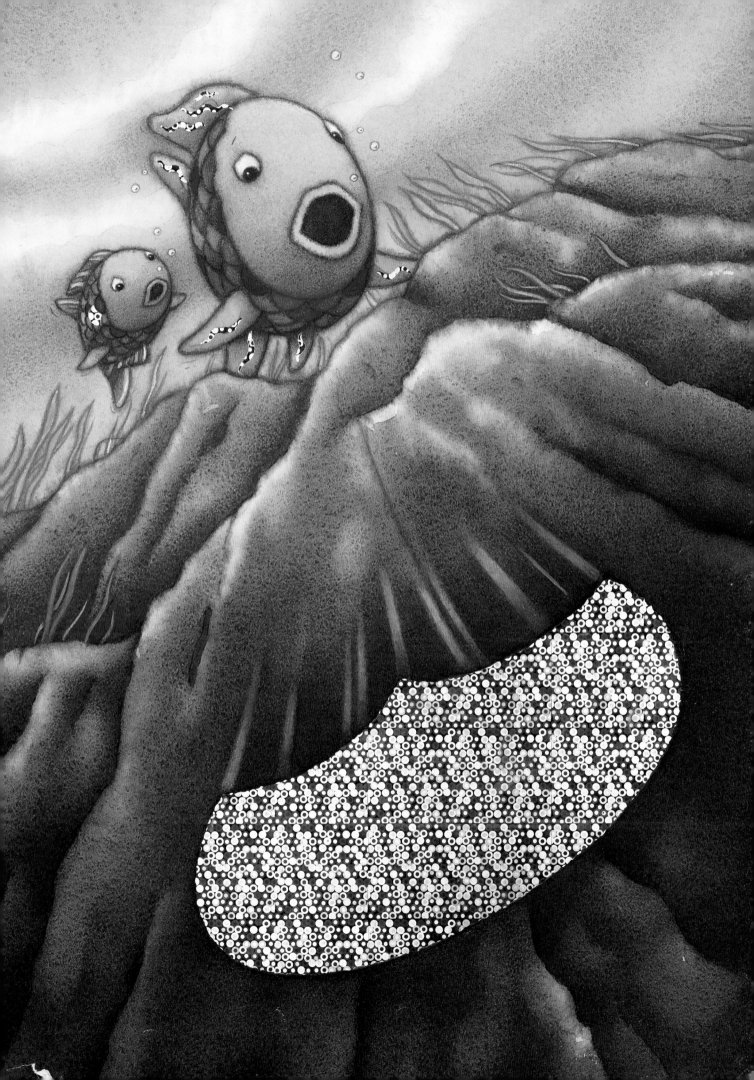

"Oh, dear," said the little blue fish. "Wait here. I'll get help."

But Rainbow Fish couldn't wait. As soon as his friend left, he dove down into the depths. He just *had* to find his scale.

Soon it was so dark that Rainbow Fish could see nothing except a tiny sparkling speck getting smaller and smaller and smaller below him. Rainbow Fish started to feel frightened.

Then suddenly it began to get light again. A glowing pink creature seemed to appear out of nowhere.

"Hello," said the creature. "I'm a firefly squid. Who are you? And what are you doing down here?"

Rainbow Fish swam closer. "I'm Rainbow Fish," he said. "I lost my sparkling silver scale, and I came down here to find it. You haven't seen it by any chance, have you?"

"I'm afraid not," said the squid. "But I can help you look."

So Rainbow Fish and the firefly squid set off to find the lost scale. Along the way, they met three glowing jellyfish.

"A sparkling silver scale?" said the jellyfish. "Yes! One drifted by this way. We played with it for a while. Then it drifted off again. We didn't know someone had lost it. If we had known that, we would have kept it for you."

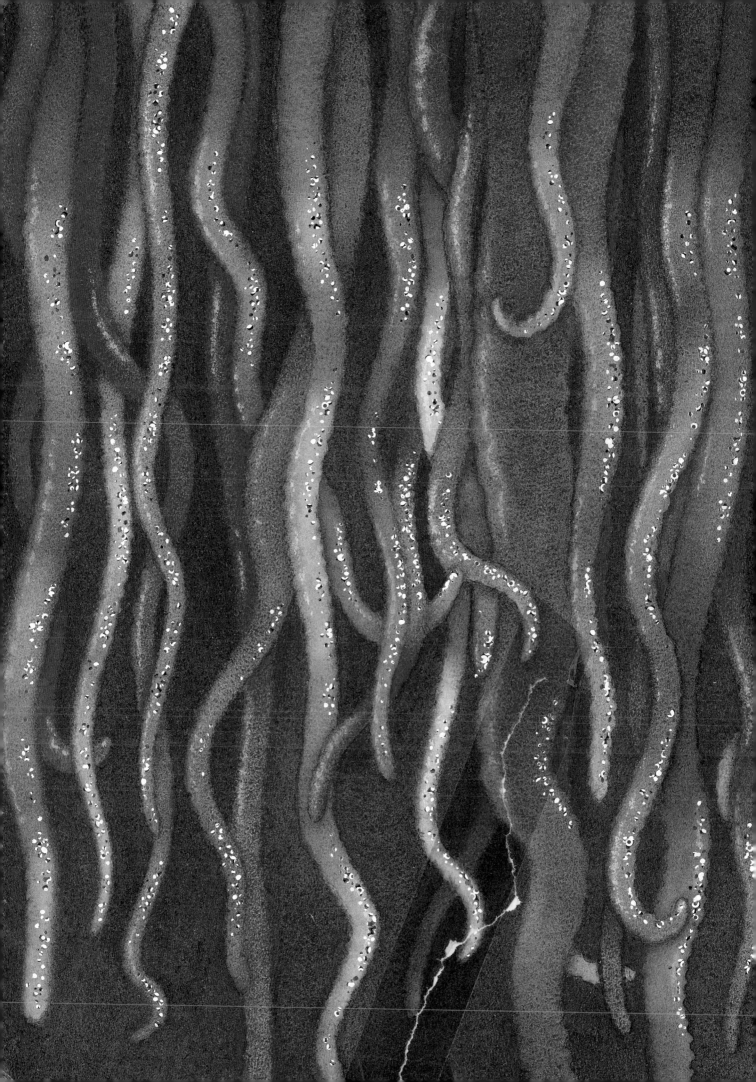

Rainbow Fish and the firefly squid swam
deeper down. Suddenly, their way was blocked by
a wavy curtain of bluish green tendrils.

"Watch out!" called the squid. "Those are the poisonous
tendrils of a siphonophore!"

Rainbow Fish shivered. There *was* danger in the deep sea.
"Have you seen my sparkling silver scale?" he asked shyly.

The siphonophore was rather rude. "Down here even the tiniest
crabs glow and glisten," he mumbled. "How can I be expected
to spot a single sparkling scale?"

"Don't feel bad," said the firefly squid. "He's just like that. Look—there's a sea slug. Maybe she's seen your scale."

But the sea slug hadn't seen anything. "Sorry," she said. "I wish I could help, but I don't see very well."

Rainbow Fish and the firefly squid swam down farther, until they reached the seabed.

"My scale must be around here somewhere," said Rainbow Fish. But it was very dark at the bottom, and the squid's light was too weak to show much.

"There's a dumbo octopus," said the firefly squid. "Come on.
I'm sure she'll help us."
But the three of them still couldn't find the sparkling scale.

"I know what to do!" cried the dumbo octopus. "I'll just give you a new sparkling costume, Rainbow Fish." And she covered him in a shower of glitter so that Rainbow Fish glistened like never before.

"Thank you!" said Rainbow Fish. "It's beautiful! Truly! But I really want my own scale back again."

"Then we're going to need more light," said the firefly squid. He called to all the creatures of the deep sea—and they all came.

Together they lit up the seabed.

"Wow!" said Rainbow Fish. "It's beautiful down here."

Then everyone looked . . . and looked . . . and looked. They were just about to give up when the light from a lantern fish showed something glittering in the water.

"My scale!" cried Rainbow Fish, and everyone cheered.

"Oh, thank you!" Rainbow Fish told his new friends. "I would never have found it without you!"

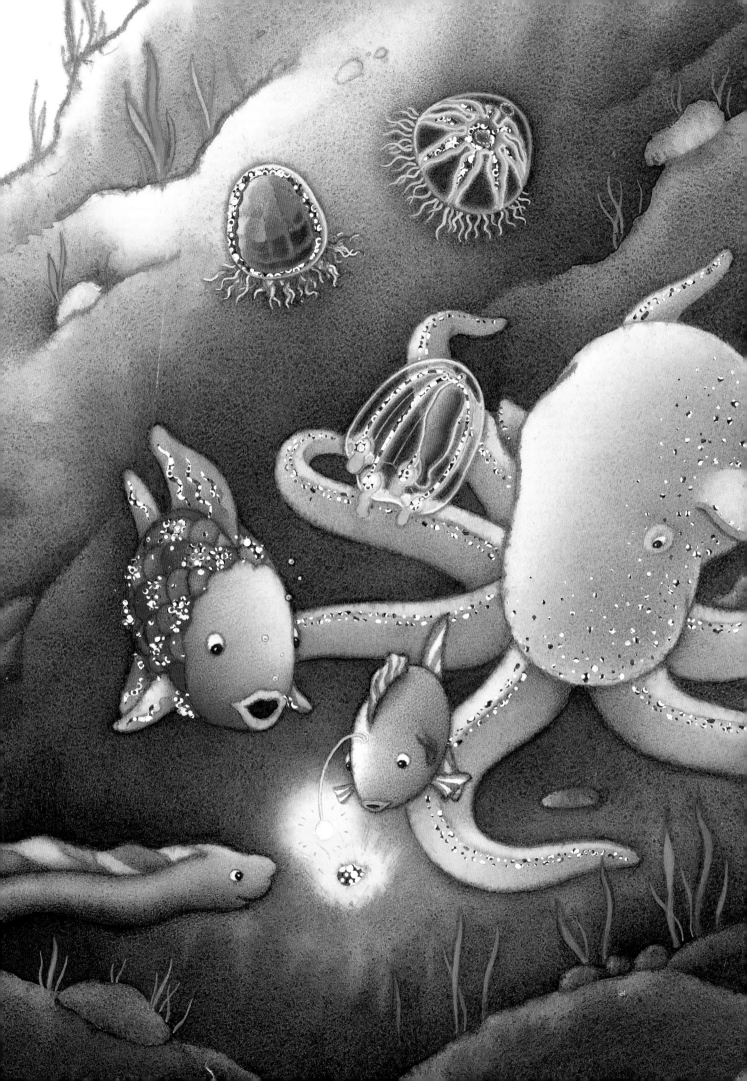

Rainbow Fish and the firefly squid swam up and up and up with the sparkling silver scale. Before they reached the top of the canyon, they had to part.

"Come visit us again," said the squid.

"I will," promised Rainbow Fish.

The little blue fish and all his other friends were waiting to welcome Rainbow Fish home. Everyone wanted to know what it was like down in the depths. "Was it scary?" they asked. "Were the creatures awful?"

"No!" said Rainbow Fish. "They were beautiful! They looked different, but they turned out to be wonderful friends. Just like you."

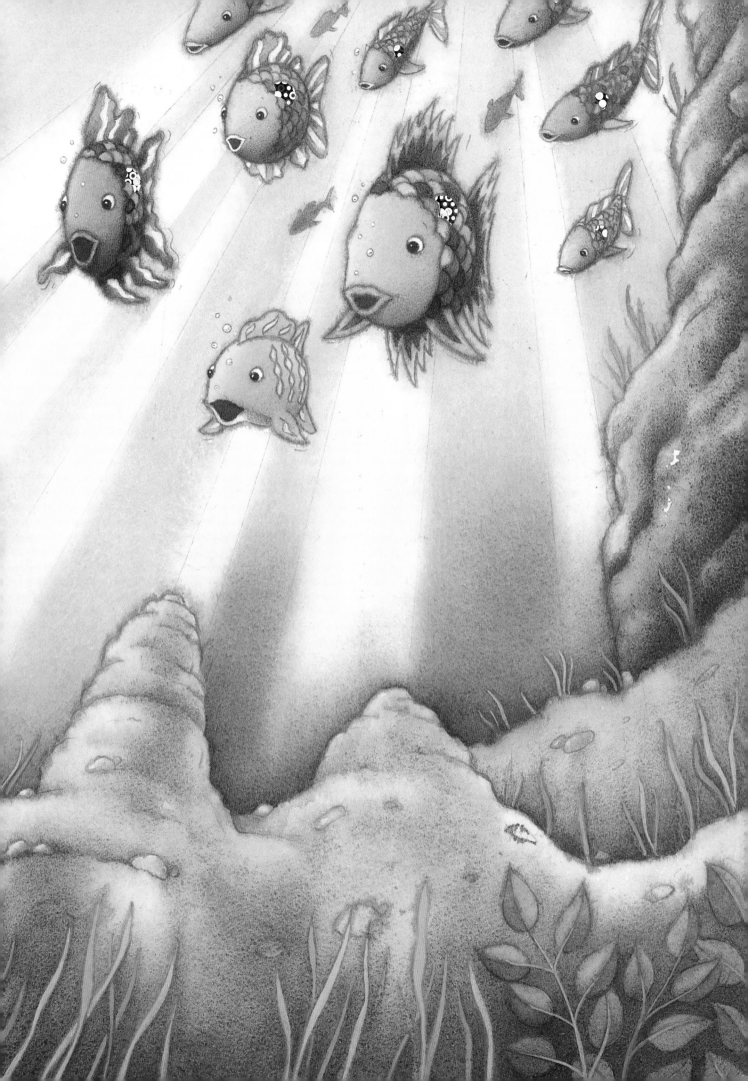

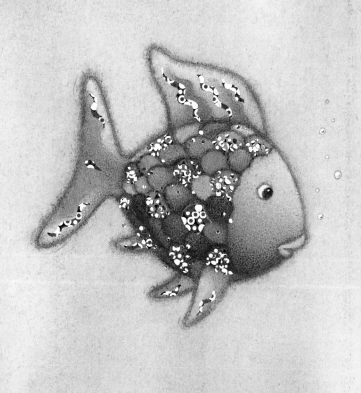

Read all the Rainbow Fish Adventures: